SADIQ
and the
Bridge
Builders

BY SIMAN NUURALI

ART BY ANJAN SARKAR

PICTURE WINDOW BOOKS
a capstone imprint

Sadiq is published by Picture Window Books, an imprint of Capstone.
1710 Roe Crest Drive
North Mankato, Minnesota 56003
www.capstonepub.com

Library of Congress Cataloging-in-Publication Data is available on the
Library of Congress website.

ISBN: 978-1-5158-7103-3 (hardcover)
ISBN: 978-1-5158-7135-4 (eBook pdf)
ISBN: 978-1-5158-7289-4 (paperback)

Summary: Lately it seems to be raining all the time, making it hard for
Sadiq to play outside. When the librarian at his school starts a building
club, Sadiq and his friends are excited to join. Inspired by the flooding
in their own neighborhood, they decide to build a model city that can
survive a natural disaster. Can Sadiq and the Bridge Builders come up
with a solution?

Image Credits
Design Element: Shutterstock/Irtsya

Designer: Brann Garvey

Printed in the United States of America.
3342

TABLE OF CONTENTS

FACTS ABOUT SOMALIA

- Somali people come from many different clans.
- Many Somalis are nomadic. That means they travel from place to place. They search for water, food, and land for their animals.
- Somalia is mostly desert. It doesn't rain often there.
- The camel is an important animal to Somali people. Camels can survive a long time without food or water.
- Around ninety-nine percent of all Somalis are Muslim.

SOMALI TERMS

baba (BAH-baah)—a common word for father

hooyo (HOY-yoh)—mother

qalbi (KUHL-bee)—my heart

salaam (sa-LAHM)—a short form of Arabic greeting, used by many Muslims. It also means "peace."

wiilkeyga (wil-KAY-gaah)—my son

CHAPTER 1

BUILDING CLUB

Sadiq was in his rain gear. He, Aliya, and his friend Zaza were walking to the bus stop.

"Ugh!" said Zaza. "I hate all this rain. When will it stop?"

"I'm not sure. I think it is supposed to rain all week," said Aliya. "It's only Monday."

"I miss playing soccer," said Sadiq sadly. "It's been too wet to play outside."

"Me too!" said Zaza. "I am bored with playing video games." He kicked a pebble on the sidewalk.

"You might have to keep playing them," said Aliya. "It doesn't look like the rain will stop soon."

The kids cut through the park. The path beside the river was flooded.

"It looks like the river is flooding," said Aliya. She tried to step around the big puddles.

Uh oh, thought Sadiq. He thought about all the rain they'd had lately. He'd heard his parents talk about something called flash floods. *I hope this flood isn't too serious,* he thought as he followed Aliya's footsteps around the puddle.

The bus ride to school was quick but rainy. At school, Sadiq and Zaza walked to their lockers to put away their things.

"Hi, Manny!" said Sadiq as he walked by his friend's locker.

"Hi, Sadiq! Hi, Zaza!" replied Manny.

The three friends walked to class together while listening to morning announcements.

"Good morning, everyone!" said Principal Turner over the speaker. "Mrs. Heisel, our school librarian, is starting a Blockos Building Club. She will hold a welcome meeting during lunch today."

"A building club?" asked Manny, looking at his friends.

"I love Blockos!" said Zaza. "Should we check it out?"

"We can't play outside anyway, so I think we should go. It would be fun to join a new club!" Sadiq said.

Mrs. Heisel stood at the door to the library during lunch. "Welcome, everyone! Please take a seat," she said.

Sadiq, Zaza, and Manny walked to one of the tables. They sat down with their lunches. Several other kids walked in after them.

When everyone was in their seats, Mrs. Heisel said, "For our first project, we will split into two teams of six. Each team will build a model city strong enough to withstand a natural disaster. Our world is changing. We have to build cities that can handle bad weather."

"What will we use to build them?" asked a girl named Lydia.

"You will use plastic building blocks called Blockos," Mrs. Heisel said. "They are a lot of fun! You can also use clay to help you with your projects. I want you all to get creative."

Zaza raised his hand. "When will we meet?" he asked.

"Twice a week after school, on Mondays and Wednesdays," said Mrs. Heisel. "Our first official meeting will be this Wednesday. The library is also going to be open at lunchtime each day. You can come and work on your projects then."

"How will we learn how to build the cities?" asked Sadiq.

"You can find instructions for building cities out of Blockos online," said Mrs. Heisel. "You will want to build houses, streets, railroads, schools, trees, and a number of other things that you find in a city. But you need to make sure you build them so they withstand a natural disaster."

"Where do we go online?" asked a boy named Zuber.

"I'll have a list of websites you can visit at our next meeting," Mrs. Heisel said. "In the meantime, think about planning your city. Also think about what natural disaster you want to protect it from. Can anyone give me an example of a natural disaster?"

Maybe we can build a city that won't flood, thought Sadiq. He raised his hand. "Flooding," he said.

"Earthquakes," said a girl named Halah.

"Hurricanes," said Zaza.

"Those are all correct," Mrs. Heisel said. "At our next meeting, we will settle on two natural disasters to protect against. One for each of the two teams."

"How long do we have to work on our projects?" asked Manny.

"Plan to have your projects done in two weeks." said Mrs. Heisel. "I invited an engineer to visit next Monday. You can ask Ms. Jessie for help then. She will judge the cities two weeks from today."

"What's an engineer?" asked Zaza.

"An engineer is someone who helps design and build things. Some engineers plan cities," said Mrs. Heisel.

Sadiq grinned. He couldn't wait to get started on his model city.

WHAT
ARE YOU

CHAPTER 2

THE FLOOD

"*Salaam*, Hooyo!" Sadiq said as he hung up his raincoat. He walked into the kitchen.

"Salaam, *wiilkeyga*," Hooyo replied. "How was your day?"

"Wet," said Sadiq, sighing.

"You're tired of the rain, aren't you?" asked Hooyo, smiling.

"Yes, Hooyo," said Sadiq.

"Did you do anything fun inside today?" asked Hooyo.

"Mrs. Heisel started a building club. Manny, Zaza, and I signed up," said Sadiq. "We get to build model cities!"

"That's wonderful, Sadiq!" said Hooyo.

Sadiq nodded. He wanted to get started planning his model city. "Have you seen my drawing kit?" he asked his mom.

"I think it's in a box down in the basement," said Hooyo. "You can go and check."

Sadiq went downstairs. He jumped off the last step—straight into a puddle!

"AHH!" shouted Sadiq. He looked down at his feet. "Why is there water in the basement?"

He ran back upstairs. "Hooyo!" said Sadiq. "There is water in the basement!"

"What?" replied Hooyo. "Water? Are you sure?"

"Yes, Hooyo! I stepped in it!" said Sadiq.

Hooyo quickly followed Sadiq downstairs.

"Go get your baba," she said once she had seen the puddle. "He is home early today. Please get Nuurali and Aliya too."

Sadiq called for his family members. Designing his model city would have to wait. In a few minutes, Sadiq, Baba, Nuurali, and Aliya had all come downstairs.

"I think it's from all the rain!" said Hooyo.

"And the melting snow," said Baba. "The ground outside is soaked with water."

Hooyo sighed. "What will we do?" she asked.

"Let's try to clean up as much as we can," said Baba. "Aliya, please go upstairs and get towels and buckets. Nuurali, bring down the fan from my office. Sadiq, help me move this table out of the water."

Sadiq helped his baba. In a few minutes, Nuurali returned with the fan. Aliya came back with more supplies.

"Baba, do you want me to mop the water?" asked Aliya. She had buckets, towels, and two mops.

"Yes, *qalbi*," said Baba. "You can twist out the water into the buckets. Sadiq and I can help you."

What a mess, Sadiq thought. He took a mop from his sister. *Good thing my model city will protect against flooding!*

* * *

On Wednesday after school, Sadiq went to the library for Building Club. After helping his family clean up, he'd gotten his drawing kit. He'd started planning his model city and had even added a bridge. He couldn't wait to show his friends.

"Hi, Mrs. Heisel!" Sadiq said as he walked in.

"Hi, Sadiq! How have you been?" asked Mrs. Heisel.

"Good. But our basement flooded on Monday," replied Sadiq.

"Oh no! I hope it wasn't too bad," said Mrs. Heisel.

"We all helped clean up," said Sadiq. "But I think it's still flooding."

"I am sorry to hear that," said Mrs. Heisel.

"It made me sure of my idea, though. Could one of the cities be protected against flooding?" said Sadiq.

Mrs. Heisel nodded. "Let's see what the rest of the group thinks."

Sadiq went to sit down with Zaza and Manny. They had just walked into the library.

When all twelve kids were gathered in the library, Mrs. Heisel spoke to them.

"Sadiq has suggested one of the cities tackle flooding. Would anyone else like work on that?" Mrs. Heisel asked.

Zaza, Manny, and three other students raised their hands.

"Perfect!" said Mrs. Heisel. "Now we just need to settle on a natural disaster for the second group."

"How about a city built for an earthquake?" said Zuber.

"I like that idea!" said Mrs. Heisel. "Does everyone agree?"

The rest of the kids nodded. They decided to join Zuber's group.

Sadiq and his group sat at a table together. "I started planning the model city. And I made a drawing of a bridge," said Sadiq. "Do you guys want to see?"

"Yes!" said Zaza and Manny.

Lydia, Halah, and Kelly nodded. They were the other students in the group.

Sadiq took out his drawing. The bridge had several tall posts to hold it up over the water. Sadiq had drawn it so it arched over a river. He had started to draw buildings along the riverbanks.

"Cool!" said Halah.

"We could definitely build this," said Kelly.

Lydia nodded. "But first I think our team needs a name," she said. She took out a notebook to write down their ideas.

"How about the Bridge Builders?" asked Manny.

Everyone agreed. They decided to split up their tasks so they could get more work done.

Sadiq and Zaza worked on the bridge and river. Kelly and Lydia worked on houses and other buildings. Manny and Halah worked on roads, sidewalks, and streets.

The kids worked hard for the rest of the meeting. They continued working on their city over lunch on Thursday. Soon they had a small model city. Now they would have to test it for flooding.

CHAPTER 3

TESTING THE MODEL

Zaza looked down at their model. It was Friday at lunchtime. "The bridge does not look high enough," he said.

"You're right. It looks too close to the water right now. Let's put a few more blocks under it. Then it will be higher over the water," said Halah.

"That's a good idea, Halah," said Sadiq. "Then we can pour the water and test it."

Kelly picked up a bottle of water and handed it to Sadiq. "Mrs. Heisel says the city will have to protect against at least one liter of water," she said. "We have to pour it at the start of the river."

Before they poured the water, the Bridge Builders put the model city into a plastic tub to keep the water from dripping everywhere.

Sadiq opened the bottle and began pouring.

"Oh no!" said Lydia. "The water is getting into the houses!"

"We have to raise the river banks higher," said Manny.

The kids used the Blockos to build the river walls higher.

"Try pouring the water again," said Zaza.

When Sadiq tried again, the water still leaked into the houses.

"How is it getting in?" said Zaza, shaking his head.

"It's getting in through the cracks in the Blockos!" said Kelly.

Sadiq shook his head sadly. "Our model is not strong enough for the floods."

"Maybe we can talk to the engineer, Ms. Jessie, on Monday," said Manny. "We can ask her what to do."

"That's a good idea," said Zaza. "She can help us figure out why the model doesn't work."

The kids dumped the water from the tub into the sink. Then they put their model city away in the storage area.

"Goodbye, Mrs. Heisel!" the kids called as they left the library.

* * *

The basement at Sadiq's house was still wet that weekend. He and his family spent part of the weekend cleaning up the mess.

"Aliya, can you grab the towels out of the dryer?" asked Hooyo.

"Yes, Hooyo," replied Aliya.

"I'll try to figure out where the water is coming in," said Baba. "In the meantime, we still need to run this fan to help dry it out."

Nuurali helped Baba move things away from the water.

"This area has been dry for two days," said Nuurali. He pointed to a corner of the basement. "I think we can store some boxes here."

Aliya came back downstairs. "Here are the towels," she said. "Sadiq, will you help me mop?"

Sadiq picked up a mop and went to help his sister.

He and his family worked very hard that weekend to keep the basement dry. But no matter how much they mopped, the water didn't go away entirely.

Sadiq was excited. It was Monday, which meant Ms. Jessie was coming to Building Club!

When the final bell rang, Sadiq, Zaza, and Manny walked together to the library.

"Hi, kids," said Mrs. Heisel, smiling. "Take your seats. We have a special guest, as promised."

"Hi, kids!" their guest said. "My name is Ms. Jessie. I'm an engineer."

"Hi, Ms. Jessie!" the kids replied.

"I hear you are working on model cities. I can't wait to see them!" said Ms. Jessie. She walked over to the Bridge Builders' table.

"I don't think ours works," said Sadiq. "The water from the river keeps flooding the houses."

"Have you tried making gutters for the water to go into?" asked Ms. Jessie. "They help direct the water where you want."

"No, we haven't," said Sadiq. "We didn't know how to make them."

"We can learn together!" Ms. Jessie said, smiling. "We can make them out of clay."

"How do we build one?" asked Sadiq.

"Here, I will show you a video," said Ms. Jessie. "It's not too hard to do once you know how."

Sadiq and Manny grabbed a tub of clay. As they watched the video, they began to shape clay into gutters.

"The water is flowing down a hill," said Ms. Jessie. "You can use gutters to control its path. They can guide the water away from the city."

"The water also leaked through the walls along the river," said Zaza. "We made them higher, but it didn't help."

"Try lining the walls with some clay," said Ms. Jessie. "It will close the cracks between the blocks. In real cities, we use cement."

Zaza took some clay from the tub. Ms. Jessie went over to the other group to help.

Zaza and Halah put the clay on the cracks between the Blockos. The rest of the Bridge Builders worked on shaping the gutters.

Soon Zaza was done patching the cracks. The others were done building the gutters.

"Try pouring some water now," said Lydia.

Zaza took a water bottle and poured the water onto the city. "Look, guys!" he said excitedly. "It's not leaking!"

Some of the water went into the gutters. But after it flowed through the gutters, the water still rushed through the model city.

Their gutters had helped a little bit, but the water still had nowhere to go. They were almost out of time.

"Oh no!" said Ms. Jessie, walking back over to Sadiq's group. "You may want to try to build a floodgate. Here are some instructions." She passed a sheet of paper to Lydia.

"Thank you, Ms. Jessie," said Lydia. "I hope this works!"

"We'll have to do it next time," said Sadiq. "We only have five minutes left in our meeting."

"Let's meet back here at lunch tomorrow," said Halah.

The rest of the team agreed and started cleaning up.

CHAPTER 4

A NEW IDEA

The next day, Lydia showed them
a picture of a floodgate. It was in the
handout that Ms. Jessie had given to
her yesterday.

"Let's try to build that," said Manny.

Each of the Bridge Builders worked
on a different part of the gate using
Blockos. Sadiq and Manny worked on
one side. Lydia and Halah got to work
on the other. Zaza and Kelly built the
posts to hold the gate in place.

When they were done, Sadiq handed the bottle of water to Lydia. "Okay, Lydia," he said. "When the gate is down, pour the water."

"I hope it works!" said Zaza.

Lydia started pouring the liter of water. Sadiq held the gate closed.

"I think it's working!" said Halah, clapping.

Sadiq tried lifting the gate a bit while Lydia poured the water. This time the water flowed more slowly. But they still didn't have good control. The water flooded the city, just less quickly this time.

"Should we leave the gate closed?" asked Kelly.

"If we leave the gate closed, the water has nowhere to go," said Halah. "We need to make sure the water drains."

"Lunch break is over," said Manny. "We should go back to class."

* * *

The next day, the Bridge Builders stood around their model city.

"Let's make another gate. Maybe we need to slow down the waterflow more," said Sadiq.

"Great idea!" said Kelly. "We can open one gate at a time."

The Bridge Builders all pitched in to make a second floodgate. When they were done, Halah poured the water. Lydia controlled the gates.

"This time, lift the first gate very slowly," said Manny. "Maybe the water will slow down."

It still did not work. The water slowed for a bit, but then it eventually flooded the city.

"We have to do something else," said Zaza. "This isn't working."

"Maybe if we—" started Manny.

CRASH!

"Oh no!" shouted Halah. "The bridge! It fell!"

"What happened?" said Manny, his hand on his head.

"I am not sure," said Halah. "I might have brushed against it. It was an accident!"

"The bridge isn't broken. It just fell down. We can put it back together the way it was," said Sadiq.

"Let's clean up and go home," said Manny. "We can work on fixing it tomorrow."

"Maybe we can also come up with another idea to solve the flooding problem by then," said Sadiq, but he was out of ideas.

* * *

Sadiq looked for his mom when he got home. He found her working in the garden.

"Salaam, Hooyo," said Sadiq.

"Salaam, qalbi," said Hooyo. "How was your day?"

"Not great," said Sadiq sadly. "Our model city failed. We couldn't stop the flooding. The bridge fell."

"Oh, I am sorry, qalbi," said Hooyo. "You weren't able to fix it?"

Sadiq shook his head. "Not yet."

"Would you like to help me in the garden?" asked Hooyo. "Maybe you'll get an idea from this."

"What are you working on?" asked Sadiq.

"I want some of the rainwater to flow to this garden here. It's called a rain garden. Hopefully the water won't flood into the basement this way," said Hooyo.

"How did you do that?" said Sadiq.

"Well, I dug a lower area right here. I directed the water here with gutters. The plants I'm putting in like the wet soil. They will soak up the rainwater," said Hooyo.

"That's a great idea, Hooyo!" said Sadiq.

Sadiq and his mom worked together until dinner.

As he dug and planted and put down mulch, Sadiq thought about his model city. *Could the Bridge Builders do something like this for our city?* he wondered.

CHAPTER 5

THE FINAL TEST

"I have an idea!" Sadiq said as he walked into the library. It was Friday during lunch. The rest of the Bridge Builders had just finished putting the bridge back up.

"We've tried everything!" said Zaza, slumping in his chair. "Ms. Jessie is coming on Monday. We don't have enough time left to solve the flooding problem."

"Zaza's right," said Halah, nodding. "No matter what we do, it keeps flooding."

"Let's at least listen to Sadiq's idea," said Kelly. "It might help us."

"I helped my mom yesterday in her garden. Our basement has been flooding," Sadiq said. "My mom changed the path of the water."

"We haven't tried that yet," said Zaza.

"Hooyo also made a rain garden," said Sadiq excitedly. "The water flows to the garden instead of into our basement."

"What's a rain garden?" asked Lydia.

"A garden that holds rainwater," said Sadiq. "Now our basement isn't flooding. And Hooyo's garden is watered!"

"You want to do the same thing for our city?" asked Zaza.

"We can make a pond for our city," said Sadiq.

A few of the club members looked uncertain.

"Let's try," said Manny. "It might work. Tell us what to do, Sadiq."

"Let's direct the gutters toward this open area. This is where a pond can hold the rainwater," said Sadiq.

The Bridge Builders worked all afternoon. Finally, they were ready to test their new system.

"Okay, Zaza," said Manny. He was
ready to control the floodgate. "Pour
the water slowly."

Zaza poured the water, and Manny
slowly lifted the floodgate.

"Is it working?" asked Halah,
covering her face. "I can't look."

Sadiq watched the water move easily through the gutters toward the pond. It collected there, leaving the city dry. The homes, streets, and buildings were protected from the flood!

"It's working!" shouted Sadiq.

* * *

Sunday afternoon was bright and sunny. Sadiq and his siblings had spent all day Saturday cleaning the basement.

"Hooyo!" called Sadiq. "I think the basement is finally dry!"

"Really?" replied Hooyo, walking down the stairs. "You're right! It is dry."

"Do you think it will flood again?" asked Sadiq.

"I hope not," said Hooyo. "Let's go check the rain garden."

They went outside together.

"Look at the water," said Sadiq. "It's flowing around the garden!"

Hooyo smiled. "And there are no more puddles around the house."

"Your idea helped me with my project, Hooyo," said Sadiq. "We couldn't fix our model city until I saw your rain garden."

"That's great, Sadiq!" said Hooyo. "Shall we go tell Baba my rain garden is working?"

"Yes!" Sadiq said. He ran back into the house.

* * *

On Monday afternoon, the children went to the library. Ms. Jessie had come to test the models. She walked around, taking notes.

"Do you think she will like ours?" asked Halah.

"I hope so," said Sadiq, biting his lip. "We worked really hard on it!"

"Well, children," said Ms. Jessie when she was done testing the projects. "I am very proud of all of you. These are great models. You should be proud too!"

The kids cheered.

"Are you ready for your next project?" asked Mrs. Heisel. "Try to build a bridge that can bear the most weight."

"Should we do it, Bridge Builders?" asked Sadiq. He looked at his friends and smiled.

"If we can keep it from falling," said Halah, grinning.

"I think we can!" said Sadiq.

GLOSSARY

cement (suh-MENT)—a gray powder made from crushed limestone and clay

design (di-ZYN)—the shape or style of something

earthquake (UHRTH-kwayk)—the sudden shaking of the earth's surface

engineer (en-juh-NEER)—a person who uses science and math to plan, design, or build

flash flood (FLASH FLUHD)—a flood that happens with little or no warning, often during periods of heavy rainfall

floodgate (FLUHD-gayt)—a gate that controls the flow of water

gutter (GUHT-ur)—a shallow channel on the edge of a road or a roof that helps water drain

hurricane (HUR-uh-kane)—a very large storm with high winds and rain

liter (LEE-tur)—a unit of measurement in the metric system equal to about 1.1 quarts

model (MOD-uhl)—identical but smaller

natural disaster (NACH-ur-uhl di-ZAS-tuhr)—an earthquake, flood, storm, or other deadly event caused by nature

protect (pruh-TEKT)—to guard or keep safe from harm

rain garden (RAYN GAHR-duhn)—a sunken garden area that collects rainwater from gutters, roofs, streets, etc.

TALK ABOUT IT

1. Pick one character from the book and discuss why you would like to have him or her as a friend.

2. Explain the problem Sadiq and the Bridge Builders are having with their model city. What would your advice be for solving the problem?

3. How did Hooyo help Sadiq solve the flooding problem in his model city? Discuss using examples from the text.

WRITE IT DOWN

1. Sadiq and his friends must build a model city to withstand a natural disaster. Pick a natural disaster that you would like to learn more about. Write a paragraph or two about what you learn.

2. The Bridge Builders work together to complete their project. How did they use teamwork to build their model city? Give a few examples from the text.

3. Draw a picture of what you imagine the Bridge Builders' model city to look like. Show where the water flows using a blue crayon or marker.

DRAW YOUR NEIGHBORHOOD

Sadiq drew a plan for his model city before he and the Bridge Builders started constructing it. Draw a map of your own city or neighborhood from a bird's-eye view.

WHAT YOU NEED:

- paper
- writing utensil
- markers, crayons, or colored pencils

WHAT TO DO:

1. Pretend you are a bird looking down on your town or neighborhood. What do you see?

2. Decide what area you want to include on your map. Do you want to include just your neighborhood? Or do you want to include a bigger area, such as a whole town or city? Or maybe you want to make up an entirely new place!

3. Brainstorm what's in your city or neighborhood.

4. Write a list of all the places you want to include on your map. Think about including buildings such as stores, hospitals, fire stations, schools, houses, apartments, and community centers. Next, consider what other things you want to include on your map: trees, rivers, lakes, mountains, parks, or oceans.

5. Once you have a good idea of what to include, start drawing. Use different colors of markers, crayons, or colored pencils to help show the different parts of your map. Maybe parks are green, water is blue, and buildings are brown. Pick the colors that make sense to you!

6. Label the places on your map.

7. Include drawings of the people, animals, and plants that live there.

8. Using your map as a guide, take a friend on a tour of your neighborhood, pointing out your favorite places.

CREATORS

Siman Nuurali grew up in Kenya. She now lives in Minnesota. Siman and her family are Somali—just like Sadiq and his family! She and her five children love to play badminton and board games together. Siman works at Children's Hospital, and in her free time, she also enjoys writing and reading.

Anjan Sarkar is a British illustrator based in Sheffield, England. Since he was little, Anjan has always loved drawing stuff. And now he gets to draw stuff all day for his job. Hooray! In addition to the Sadiq series, Anjan has been drawing mischievous kids, undercover aliens, and majestic tigers for other exciting children's book projects.